THE CHOSEN PROTECTORS

THE CLASH WITH THE ASURAS

ANIKETH VINOD BHAT

Contents

Contents

Disclaimer

This is a work of fiction. Unless otherwise indicated, all the names, characters, places, events, and incidents in this book are either the product of the author's imagination or used in a fictitious manner. Any resemblance to actual persons, living or dead, or actual events is purely coincidental.

CHAPTER ONE

DISCOVERING A LIFE'S TRUE PURPOSE

In the life of Akash, every day used to follow a predictable routine. He went to college, attended lectures, read textbooks, and enjoyed the company of his friends. His world was all about academics and friendships, where the pursuit of knowledge was the main focus. The mysteries of existence felt distant and unimportant. Little did he know that a day would come, a day that would change his life forever.

It all began with an unusual and deep sleep. It was so profound that it felt like it could bridge the gap between the mortal and divine realms, blending them together. In this strange dream, Akash found himself in the presence of celestial beings— the Trimurti—Brahma, Vishnu, and Shiva. These beings represented creation, preservation and destruction, and their radiance illuminated the universe. Lord Shiva, the destroyer, and regenerator of worlds, spoke to Akash. His voice carried the weight of prophecy, echoing through time itself. The words he spoke were not just words; they were threads that wove the fabric of destiny.

"Akash," Lord Shiva began, "the asuras, ancient malevolent demons, have awoken from their ancient slumber. They threaten to engulf the world in darkness once more. You, my mortal vessel, are chosen to undertake a sacred mission—to gather an army capable of standing against these malevolent forces."

Akash was overwhelmed by a mix of emotions—awe, humility, and a profound sense of duty. He couldn't help but question the divine beings. The task ahead seemed impossible. "How can I, a mere mortal, face such formidable adversaries?" he asked, his voice trembling with both doubt and determination.

In response, Lord Shiva unfolded a celestial map, a tapestry of constellations and mystical markings that shimmered with cosmic energy. This map revealed the hidden location of Arjuna's legendary bow, Gandiva, and quiver. These artifacts, thought to be lost to history, held unmatched power and were the key to their mission. Their mission would not only determine the fate of their world but also the balance of the entire universe.

As he gazed upon the celestial map, Akash's doubt began to fade. It was replaced by a sense of purpose and determination. The divine had chosen him and provided the means to fulfil this extraordinary destiny. He accepted the responsibility, knowing he was embarking on a quest that would push the limits of his mortal existence and take him to the edge of the divine.

From that moment, Akash's life took on a new meaning. College and its mundane concerns faded into the background as he embraced his newfound purpose. He knew the journey ahead would be filled with challenges and dangers, but he was willing to face them all. He had been chosen to be a beacon of hope in a world threatened by darkness. As he prepared to leave behind the ordinary world, Akash felt the weight of destiny on his shoulders. It had awakened in him a profound sense of purpose. With the celestial map in hand and the blessings of the Trimurti, he embarked on a path that would lead to unimaginable adventures, mortal and divine allies, and a destiny that would forever change his life and the fate of the universe itself.

CHAPTER TWO

UNITING FORCES

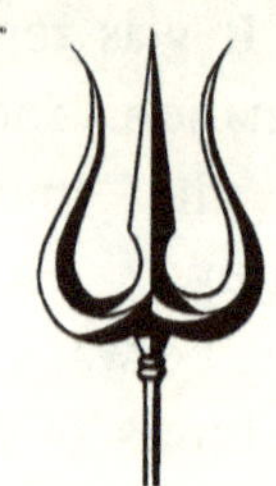

The Call of Friendship and Destiny

Akash's encounter with the divine left him in deep contemplation. The message he received in his dream was not something he could simply dismiss. It was a call from forces beyond human comprehension, a powerful conviction that stirred within him as if a celestial fire had been ignited.

Amid this spiritual awakening, Akash realized that he couldn't embark on the incredible journey that lay before him alone. He needed the support and companionship of those he trusted most in the world. And so, with unwavering determination, he reached out to his dearest friends: Karthik, Preeti, and Tara.

As they gathered at his humble abode, their faces were alight with anticipation. Akash began to share the astonishing revelation that had unfolded in his dream.

The words of the Trimurti, the divine beings symbolizing the essence of creation, preservation, and destruction, were etched in his memory like a sacred mantra. His friends listened with rapt attention, their eyes filled with wonder and awe.

The weight of their mission, the destiny of the entire world resting on their shoulders, hung heavily in the air. It was a responsibility that could have overwhelmed even the strongest of individuals. Yet, in that moment, an unbreakable bond formed among them. It was a bond forged not only through friendship but also through their shared determination to answer the divine call.

They understood that they were chosen for a purpose that extended far beyond their own lives, a purpose that transcended the boundaries of mortal existence. It was a purpose that demanded not only sacrifice and courage but also unwavering commitment.

Together, they stood on the precipice of an extraordinary journey, one that would take them far beyond the realm of the ordinary and into the domain of the divine. The realization of the enormity of their task sank in. They knew that their journey would be filled with challenges, dangers, and moments that would test the very core of their beings.

With their hearts united in purpose, they embarked on this sacred quest, ready to confront whatever challenges lay ahead. The path before them was shrouded in uncertainty, and the malevolent forces they would confront were ancient, formidable, and malevolent. Yet, their conviction burned brighter than ever. They believed they were destined to play a pivotal role in a cosmic drama, a story that had been written in the stars and whispered to them in the depths of their souls.

As they set out on their journey, they carried not only the celestial map that would lead them to Arjuna's legendary bow and quiver but also an unshakable belief in their friendship, shared purpose, and the divine guidance they had received.

Bound by destiny, they stood as a beacon of hope in a world threatened by darkness, determined to confront the malevolent forces that had awakened and, in doing so, to restore balance to the universe.

Theirs was a journey of epic proportions, filled with challenges, mysteries, and the unwavering bonds of friendship, all of which would be revealed in the chapters yet to come.

CHAPTER THREE

THE QUEST BEGINS

Trials and Asuras

As they continued on their quest, following the celestial map that seemed to pulse with otherworldly energy, they were drawn to the serene shores of the Arabian Sea. This location was a remarkable blend of natural beauty and an underlying sense of foreboding. The sea's gentle waves kissed the shore, reflecting the fading sunlight, but there was an intangible tension in the air, as if the very elements of the world were aware of the impending conflict.

At this juncture, where land met sea, they began to sense the lurking malevolence, a sign of the formidable challenges that lay ahead. This malevolence cast a palpable darkness over the otherwise serene landscape. The group exchanged cautious glances, silently acknowledging the gravity of their mission and the dangers, they were about to face.

Weaker evil forces, mere minions of the ancient and malevolent asuras, dared to confront them. Karthik and Akash, who had diligently and faithfully performed their daily Sandhyavandana rituals, found themselves drawing upon the spiritual power they had cultivated over time. Their newfound strength, a fusion of their unwavering commitment and spiritual devotion, coursed through their veins as they faced the lesser asuras.

They were not prepared for it. So, it took a very big toll on their body. The next moment They both fell down due to sheer exhaustion, fluttering into the depths of unconsciousness.

These clashes with the lesser asuras were but a prelude to the epic confrontation they knew awaited them. The battles were intense and draining, each clash testing their physical and spiritual mettle. Yet, they faced these adversaries with a tenacity born of their shared purpose and the profound sense of duty that had been bestowed upon them. Exhausted and battered, they pressed forward, for they understood that these early trials were a crucible, forging their resolve and preparing them for the far greater challenges yet to come.

As the sun dipped below the horizon, casting long, elongated shadows across the shoreline, Akash began to slowly regain consciousness. He found himself resting with his head cradled in Preeti's lap. Worry lines etched her face as she kept a vigilant watch over him, her unwavering determination mirroring the resolve of their entire group. Nearby, Karthik remained unconscious, his body still recovering from the toll of their recent battle.

Amidst the exhaustion and uncertainty that permeated the air, one thing was undeniable—their determination to fulfil their mission burned brighter than ever. It was a shared commitment that transcended the physical and spiritual challenges they faced. Their bond, forged in the crucible of adversity, remained unbreakable, and they knew that, as long as their purpose held strong, they could weather any storm and face any foe on their path to safeguarding their world from the encroaching darkness.

In the moments of respite that followed, they renewed their vow to each other and to the divine. They understood that their journey was far from over, and the trials they had faced were but the first steps on a path that would lead them deeper into the heart of an ancient and cosmic battle. With the celestial map as their guide and their unwavering friendship as their strength, they steeled themselves for what lay ahead, ready to confront the malevolent asuras and restore balance to a world teetering on the edge of darkness.

CHAPTER FOUR

A MOMENT OF RESPITE

Bonding and Reflection

In the wake of a battle that seemed to stretch on for an eternity, Karthik gradually roused from the depths of unconsciousness. His eyelids fluttered open, revealing a campsite that bore the lingering marks of their recent skirmish. The air still carried the echoes of the battle, and his senses tingled with the remnants of that fierce engagement. It was Tara's steady and comforting presence that enabled him to sit up, though his body felt unsteady, and his strength was slowly returning.

As the sun descended below the horizon, their determination pushed them forward in their search for Arjuna's lost bow and quiver. The dense forest enveloped them, its ancient trees whispering enigmatic secrets with every rustle in the breeze. Sinister forces lurked in the shadows, an ever-present reminder of the perils that surrounded them.

With evening approaching and the fading light complicating their search, they decided to make a practical choice and conclude their efforts for the day. They recognized that rest was not a luxury but an absolute necessity. Their arduous journey was far from over, and they needed all their strength and wits about them to confront the formidable challenges awaiting them.

In a small clearing, they established their camp. The campfire's flames cast a mesmerizing dance of shadows upon their faces. Around the comforting warmth of the fire, they shared tales of their past exploits, reminiscing about the trials they had conquered and the daunting ones that loomed in their future. Each story served as a testament to their unwavering resolve and indomitable spirit.

Their bonds as friends and comrades grew stronger with each passing moment. In the flickering light of the campfire and the tranquil ambiance of the forest, they discovered solace in the unity of their purpose and the unbreakable camaraderie that bound them together. These shared moments of reflection and connection not only refreshed their spirits but also fortified their determination to face the challenges yet to come.

Beneath the expansive canvas of stars that stretched across the night sky, they sat in contemplative silence. The campfire's crackling served as a soothing backdrop to their thoughts. In this hushed stillness, they keenly felt the gravity of their destiny and the profound responsibility that rested on their shoulders. However, they also drew strength from each other's presence, their shared determination acting as a beacon of hope against the encroaching darkness.

As they settled in for the night, their dreams were filled with visions of their mission and the formidable challenges that awaited. Yet, they slept with a profound sense of purpose and unity, understanding that together they possessed the capacity to achieve the extraordinary and safeguard their world from the resurrected asuras. The trials they had faced and the bonds they had forged had prepared them for what lay ahead, and they would confront it with unwavering courage, fully aware that their destiny was intricately interwoven with the very fabric of the universe.

CHAPTER FIVE

THE DIVINE DISCOVERY

Unveiling the Sacred Artifacts

As the night deepened, and their campfire crackled, casting enchanting and ever-shifting shadows upon the forest floor, it was Karthik's astute and discerning eyes that first detected an extraordinary occurrence. His gaze, like a divining rod, was irresistibly drawn to a nearby Shami tree. Nestled among its branches, he discerned a faint yet unmistakable divine aura—an ethereal radiance that seemed to beckon to them, luring them closer to its source.

A silent but profound exchange of excited glances swept through the group; a shared curiosity ignited by this inexplicable phenomenon. Without a moment's hesitation, they moved as one, their footsteps filled with eager anticipation as they approached the Shami tree. They were guided by the otherworldly presence emanating from it, drawing nearer with hearts pounding—a blend of wonder, hope, and a hint of trepidation.

Karthik, ever the steady and cautious one, approached the tree's branches with meticulous care. Guided by the celestial aura that illuminated his path, he reached for a concealed bundle nestled amid the leaves. With great reverence and care, he began to unravel the bundle, unveiling the treasures it held within.

To their absolute astonishment and awe, the bundle revealed the very legendary weapons they had been tirelessly seeking—the very artifacts that had been the linchpin of their quest and the very reason for their divine mission. Within the protective embrace of the Shami tree's branches lay Arjuna's fabled bow, Gandiva, and his quiver, filled with inexhaustible arrows. It was a moment of profound significance as if the cosmos itself had conspired to deliver these divine tools of destiny into their hands.

Beside the bow, their eyes alighted upon other legendary weapons—Nakula's sword, now safeguarded by Preeti; Vijaya bow, claimed by Karthik; and Chandrahaas, held by Tara. These treasures, like the radiant bow and quiver, were steeped in the rich mythology and legends of their world, each imbued with mystical power. It was as though they had been destined to uncover this cache of divine armaments, with each weapon representing a unique facet of their sacred journey.

With a reverence that bordered on the divine, they cradled the sacred artifacts in their hands. The weight of their newfound responsibility hung heavily in the air; a palpable reminder of the destiny that had been thrust upon them. These legendary weapons, with their storied histories and unparalleled might, would be instrumental in the impending battle against the resurrected asuras. With these treasures now in their possession, they stood one significant step closer to fulfilling their divine mission, one step closer to confronting the malevolent forces that threatened to plunge their world into darkness once more.

Their journey had led them to this pivotal moment, a moment of divine revelation and the acquisition of the tools that would empower them in their quest. As they looked at one another, their eyes filled with determination and awe, they understood that they were now truly prepared to confront the malevolent forces that awaited them. The destiny for which they had been chosen was unfolding before their very eyes, and they were ready to embrace it with unwavering courage and unwavering commitment. Their faith in the divine and in each other had grown stronger than ever before.

CHAPTER SIX

THE SEARCH FOR PARASHURAMA

Guided by Faith

The recovery of the legendary weapons was but a single facet of their divine odyssey. In the realm of dreams, Lord Brahma, one of the three divine beings of the Trimurti, unfolded a new chapter in their journey to Akash—a concealed sanctuary belonging to Parashurama, a sage of profound wisdom and a master of martial arts. This sanctuary was nestled deep within the formidable embrace of the Mahendra Giri mountains, a place of profound spiritual significance.

As they made their way toward this sacred haven, their sense of purpose deepened. The knowledge of Parashurama's abode acted as a guiding light, leading them through the rugged and perilous terrain. Guided by faith, intuition, and the ancient wisdom passed down through generations, they combed the mountainside for an unrelenting three days. The pursuit was gruelling, and the unforgiving terrain tested their resolve, but their determination never faltered.

Then, on the fourth day, it was Preeti, with her sharp and observant eye, who caught a glimpse of a faint and otherworldly light emanating from one of the cave entrances. It was a sight both subtle and profound, a beacon of hope in their relentless quest. Without a moment's hesitation, they ventured toward this alluring glow, their hearts brimming with anticipation.

As they entered the cave, they were met with a sight that left them breathless and transcendent—Lord Parashurama, a living legend, was there before them, deep in meditation upon a tiger's skin. His presence was awe-inspiring, his aura radiating wisdom and power that transcended the earthly realm. In humble reverence, they gathered around him, their spirits overcome with a profound sense of honour and privilege.

Initiating a sacred chant, "Om Parashuraamaaya Namaha," they paid homage to the sage who had devoted his life to the pursuit of martial arts and spiritual enlightenment. Time itself seemed to flow in timeless currents as they immersed themselves in meditation, the vibrations of their chant resonating through the cave.

An astonishing 18 days passed in a timeless reverie, their physical needs and the world beyond the cave forgotten in the presence of the sage. During this period of profound introspection and spiritual communion, they sought not just knowledge and power but also a deeper understanding of their own purpose and the divine mission that had brought them to this sacred place.

Then, on the 18th day, a divine voice stirred their souls, breaking the trance that had held them in its thrall. It was a voice that carried the echoes of eternity, a voice that spoke of destiny and the challenges that lay ahead. With renewed purpose and a sense of divine guidance, they emerged from the cave, ready to continue their journey, armed not only with legendary weapons but also with the spiritual wisdom and strength imparted by their encounter with Parashurama.

Their encounter with the sage had deepened their understanding of the divine mission that lay before them. As they stepped back into the world, they were filled with a profound sense of purpose and a renewed commitment to their sacred quest. The challenges ahead were formidable, but their faith and the wisdom they had gained from Parashurama would serve as their guiding light, leading them ever closer to their destiny as champions of light in a world threatened by darkness.

CHAPTER SEVEN

TRAINING UNDER PARASHURAMA

Forging Body and Spirit

With profound respect and a deep sense of purpose, Akash, as the chosen leader of their group, divulged to Parashurama the divine purpose of their quest and the looming return of the asuras—ancient malevolent demons that threatened to cast the world into darkness once more. Parashurama, the sage of profound wisdom and martial mastery, listened intently to their plea.

After careful consideration, Parashurama agreed to guide them on their mission, recognizing the gravity of their endeavour. However, he issued a solemn and weighty warning, the seriousness of which hung heavy in the air. "Remember," he cautioned, "falsehoods spoken in my presence will lead to consequences akin to Karna's fate."

Karna, a central figure in the epic of the Mahabharata, had met a tragic end due to a series of fateful and unalterable choices. He had called himself a Brahman to become a disciple of lord Parashurama. At that time Parashurama no longer thought of kshatriyas. Parashurama's reference to Karna's fate served as a stern reminder of the importance of truth, integrity, and honesty in their quest—a reminder that falsehoods could carry consequences as grave as those faced by the tragic hero of the epic.

Under the sage's tutelage, the group embarked on a gruelling regimen of training. Akash and Karthik dedicated themselves intensively to honing their archery skills to unparalleled mastery, striving to wield Arjuna's bow, Gandiva, with the precision and power that the legendary warrior himself possessed. Meanwhile, Preeti and Tara delved deep into the art of swordsmanship, their dedication unwavering as they aimed to harness the full potential of the legendary weapons they had acquired.

Eighteen months passed in a relentless blur of training and discipline. Each day began well before dawn, the first rays of sunlight bearing witness to their dedication as they embarked on their morning rituals, invoking the divine and preparing their bodies and minds for the challenges that lay ahead. Then, with unwavering focus and under the watchful eye of Parashurama, they delved into the intricacies of martial arts and weapon mastery, pushing the limits of their physical and spiritual capabilities.

Through their collective effort and shared determination, they grew not only in skill and strength but also in understanding. Their training was more than just a means to an end; it was a transformative journey that forged them into formidable warriors and individuals of unwavering integrity. As they toiled tirelessly, the wisdom imparted by Parashurama became a beacon of light, illuminating their path and strengthening their resolve for the challenges that lay ahead in their mission to protect the world from the resurrected Asuras.

With each passing day, their bond as a group grew stronger, their unwavering trust in one another bolstering their shared purpose. Parashurama's teachings, rooted in both martial expertise and spiritual wisdom, not only elevated their physical prowess but also nurtured their souls. They were no longer just individuals; they were a united force, ready to face any adversary and overcome any obstacle in their quest to safeguard their world from the encroaching darkness.

As they neared the completion of their training under the sage's guidance, they understood that they were on the cusp of a new chapter in their divine journey—a chapter that would test the full extent of their abilities and the depths of their commitment. With the wisdom of Parashurama and the bonds they had forged, they were prepared to meet whatever challenges the future held with unwavering courage and unity.

CHAPTER EIGHT

THE TRIALS OF VIRTUE

Lessons Beyond Combat

As the months evolved into seasons and their relentless training under Parashurama continued, the challenges they faced transcended the realm of the purely physical. Parashurama, a sage of profound wisdom, was not merely an expert in martial skills; he was a believer in the harmony of mind, body, and spirit. Their training regimen encompassed not only the art of combat but also the cultivation of virtue, a dimension of their journey that would prove to be as profound as their mastery of weapons.

After their arduous physical exercises each day, Parashurama would gather them under the shade of a colossal banyan tree, its ancient branches providing both shelter and wisdom. With a stern yet compassionate gaze, he would impart lessons on morality, ethics, and the path to righteousness.

"Strength without virtue is a weapon in the hands of chaos," he would solemnly remind them. "To protect this world from the impending darkness, you must not only be skilled warriors but also virtuous beings."

Under the sage's guidance, they delved deep into the scriptures, immersing themselves in the study of ancient texts and philosophies that had guided generations of warriors and sages before them. Parashurama's teachings extended far beyond the confines of the battlefield. He emphasized the importance of compassion, humility, and integrity in all aspects of life.

Their trials of virtue were as rigorous as their physical training. Parashurama tasked them with acts of kindness, compassion, and selflessness in the nearby villages, allowing them to experience firsthand the impact of their actions on the lives of others. Through these experiences, they learned the profound importance of respecting all life and treating every being with dignity, for Parashurama insisted that these lessons were the very essence of being true protectors of the world.

As they embraced these teachings of virtue, a profound transformation began to take root within them. Their hearts grew lighter, and their minds clearer, as they began to see the interconnectedness of all living beings. The bond between them, forged in the crucible of relentless physical and moral training, deepened as they shared these transformative experiences.

In the shadow of the ancient banyan tree, as the sun set and the stars emerged overhead, they came to realize that their journey was not merely about preparing for a physical battle against the asuras. It was a quest to embody the very ideals that would safeguard the world from darkness. The trials of virtue continued, and with each passing day, they grew not only as warriors but as individuals with a deep sense of purpose and an unwavering commitment to uphold the values that Parashurama had instilled in them.

Little did they know that these virtues, instilled through countless acts of compassion, humility, and selflessness, would be assessed in ways they could not yet imagine as they drew closer to their ultimate confrontation with the Asuras. The moral fortitude they had cultivated under the banyan tree would prove to be as vital as their prowess in combat in the trials that lay ahead.

CHAPTER NINE

THE DIVINE BLESSING

The Gift of Extraordinary Powers

Their relentless training under Parashurama's guidance had persisted for an unyielding 18 months, pushing them to the very precipice of their physical and spiritual capabilities. Each day was a testament to their unswerving dedication, a testament to their unwavering resolve to prepare for the impending battle against the resurrected Asuras.

On the final day of their gruelling training, as the sun cast its warm and golden glow upon the world, an ethereal moment unfolded. The Trimurti, the divine trio of Brahma, Vishnu, and Shiva, reappeared, their presence exuding both gravity and transcendence. It was a moment that transcended mortal boundaries as Lord Vishnu delivered grave tidings—the asuras would launch their attack in just two days, and the epic battleground of Kurukshetra would bear witness to this impending clash of cosmic forces.

In this moment of divine intervention, the Trimurti bestowed upon them a profound blessing—a power beyond mortal comprehension. Akash, the chosen leader, felt a surge of divine energy coursing through his being. He was now endowed with the extraordinary ability to release arrows swifter than the speed of light, wielding the formidable Brahmastra, Vaishnav Astra, and Brahmashirastra. These were not mere weapons; they were cosmic forces capable of unleashing unimaginable devastation upon their adversaries.

Preeti, with her unwavering determination and inner strength, was granted a power that defied the very laws of time itself. She could now halt time for a precious eighteen minutes, a gift that would prove invaluable in critical moments during the impending battle.

Karthik, ever the stalwart and resolute warrior, was entrusted with the sacred Armor of Karna, a legendary artifact with the power to shield its wearer from the most formidable of attacks. What made this gift even more extraordinary was Karthik's newfound ability to share this protective power with his comrades during moments of dire need.

Tara, possessing a unique blend of cunning and wisdom, was bestowed with the ability to manipulate the minds of Asuras—an invaluable tool that could turn the tide of battle. However, this power came at a draining cost, for she would have to exert immense mental energy to sway the will of these malevolent beings. There were some, she knew, with wills of iron that her powers could not easily sway.

Their training, both physical and moral, was complete. Standing at the precipice of destiny, they were now a formidable force, armed not only with legendary weapons but also with incomprehensible powers bestowed upon them by the divine. Parashurama's teachings had fortified their spirits, and they were prepared to confront the resurrected Asuras, who threatened to engulf the world in darkness once more.

The fate of the world hung in the balance as they readied themselves for the epic confrontation on the hallowed battleground of Kurukshetra. They knew that the trials they had endured, the wisdom they had gained, and the powers they now possessed would all be put to the ultimate test in the battle that awaited them—a battle that would determine

the destiny of their world and the very balance of
the cosmos itself.

CHAPTER TEN

Journey to Kurukshetra

A Test of Will and Unity

As they embarked on their journey toward Kurukshetra, the site of the impending battle with the resurrected Asuras, the anticipation of the impending conflict hung heavy in the air. Their path was not merely a physical one but a multifaceted test of their mettle, determination, and the unity of their group. The challenges they encountered along the way were as diverse as the terrain itself, demanding their unwavering resolve.

The landscape unfolded before them like an epic tale. They ventured through ancient forests, where towering trees whispered secrets of times long past. The air was heavy with the scent of earth and life, and though the beauty of nature surrounded them, they remained vigilant. They knew that lurking asuras could strike from the shadows, eager to disrupt their mission to protect humanity.

In the heart of arid deserts, they confronted the scorching sun and the relentless sands that seemed to stretch into eternity. The unforgiving heat threatened to drain their strength, but they pressed forward, drawing inspiration from the divine blessings they had received and the unwavering teachings of Parashurama. Each step they took was a testament to their determination and their unwavering commitment to the task at hand.

Their journey also led them through treacherous mountain passes, where jagged peaks seemed to pierce the very heavens. The thin air challenged their endurance, and the rugged terrain assessed their agility. Yet, they navigated these obstacles with the grace and precision instilled in them by their training under Parashurama. Each trial strengthened their bond as a group, forging them into a cohesive unit ready to face any challenge that lay ahead.

Amidst the vastness of rolling plains, they encountered nomadic tribes whose wisdom and traditions enriched their understanding of the world. Their tales of ancient battles and heroic deeds reminded them of the legacy they carried as chosen protectors, entrusted with the task of preserving the world from the impending darkness.

As they journeyed onward, they also encountered mystical beings and wise sages who shared cryptic clues about the whereabouts of the asuras and the impending battle. Each encounter was a piece of the puzzle, bringing them closer to their ultimate destination and the confrontation that would determine the fate of humanity.

Their journey to Kurukshetra was not just a physical trek but a spiritual odyssey, a test of their collective will and unity. They drew strength from one another, from the teachings of Parashurama, and from the divine blessings they had received. The fate of the world depended on their success, and as they approached the hallowed battleground of Kurukshetra, they did so with hearts filled with determination and purpose.

The stage was set, and the ultimate battle against the resurrected asuras loomed on the horizon. Akash and his companions were ready to face their destiny, armed not only with legendary weapons and extraordinary powers but also with the virtues that defined them as true protectors of the world. The epic confrontation would evaluate them in ways they could scarcely imagine, but their resolve remained unshakable as they stood together, united in purpose and ready to confront the forces of darkness.

CHAPTER ELEVEN

TRIALS AND TRIBULATIONS

The journey to Kurukshetra continued, leading the group deeper into a dense forest shrouded in an eerie stillness. Unbeknownst to them, malevolent forces had dispatched bewitched creatures, their eyes gleaming with an otherworldly malevolence, to halt their progress and thwart their mission.

Their first encounter was with a pack of enormous wolves, their fur as dark as the night and their feral instincts honed by dark magic. Preeti, ever watchful and quick to react, was the first to spot their stealthy approach. As the wolves lunged with a hunger for their destruction, she unsheathed Nakula's sword, a legendary weapon of great power, and met their aggression with a flurry of expert strokes. Her swordplay was a mesmerizing display of skill and grace, fending off the ferocious creatures.

Karthik, armed with the formidable Vijaya bow, stood his ground, his arrows flying with unparalleled precision. His shots struck true, preventing the creatures from closing in on them. Tara, possessing the unique ability to manipulate the minds of asuras, proved her worth in this dire situation. With a focused effort, she confused the wolves, sowing discord among them and making them turn on each other in a frenzy of snarls and bites.

As the wolves closed in, sensing their opportunity, Akash, the leader of their group, unleashed a rapid volley of arrows. Each arrow found its mark with unerring accuracy, and the wolves, struck with terror and unable to focus amidst the relentless barrage, faltered in their attack. Their menacing growls turned into howls of pain as they were overwhelmed by the combined might of arrows and the disorienting power of Tara's manipulation.

Through their combined efforts and the skills, they had honed under Parashurama's guidance, they triumphed over the first formidable obstacle in their path. With the wolves vanquished and their resolve unshaken, they pressed forward deeper into the heart of the enchanted forest, knowing that even greater challenges lay ahead.

But the forest held more than just enchanted beasts. Treacherous terrain awaited them, with cliffs that seemed to defy gravity and chasms that threatened to swallow them whole. It was a test of not only their strength but also their agility and resourcefulness.

In this perilous landscape, Tara's power to halt time for eighteen precious minutes proved invaluable. With her aid, they navigated the precarious terrain, each step a testament to their unwavering determination to reach their ultimate goal and confront the resurrected asuras on the battlefield of Kurukshetra.

CHAPTER TWELVE

THE ENCHANTED FOREST

Our journey through the enchanted forest had taken a toll on our group of chosen protectors. The physical and mental exhaustion from battling the water demon and the resurrected wolves weighed heavily upon us as we ventured deeper into uncharted territory.

The forest itself seemed to conspire against us, with the trees closing in like sentinels of darkness. The eerie silence was broken only by the occasional rustle of unseen creatures. We moved cautiously, our senses on high alert, knowing that malevolent forces could strike at any moment.

Preeti, ever the vigilant one, kept her hand firmly on Nakula's sword. Karthik, still clad in Karna's Armor, scanned our surroundings, his eyes sharp and unyielding. Tara, her powers evaluated to the limit, maintaining a protective barrier around us, warding off potential threats.

As they ventured deeper into the forest's heart, an unnatural mist began to envelop them. It seemed to seep into their very souls, assessing their resolve and sapping their strength. Doubts and fears crept into their minds, but they clung to the purpose that had brought them together – to protect humanity from the resurrected asuras.

Deeper into the forest, they encountered a mystical river, its waters shimmering with an unnatural glow. As they approached, a deafening roar echoed through the trees. A colossal water demon, sent by the Asuras, emerged from the depths. With a mighty sweep of its arm, it conjured a powerful whirlpool, threatening to engulf them.

Karthik, resolute in his possession of Karna's armour, took the lead. The enchanted armour transformed, shielding him from the swirling maelstrom. Preeti, with Nakula's sword, stood at the ready, her keen eyes searching for an opportunity. Tara, drawing upon her powers despite the draining cost, attempted to manipulate the water demon's mind. Their battle with the water demon raged on, each moment pushing us to the brink of exhaustion. Just when it seemed their combined might not be enough, a resurgence of malevolence erupted from the depths of the forest. The wolves they had previously vanquished, now resurrected and fuelled by vengeful fury, descended upon them from all sides.

They were surrounded, our backs against the shimmering river. With no way to escape, Akash knew it was time to unleash the Vaishnav Astra, the divine weapon granted to him by Lord Vishnu himself. With a resounding chant, He summoned its power, releasing a blinding beam of energy that surged forth to confront the onslaught of resurrected wolves.

The Vaishnav Astra's brilliance cut through the forest like a celestial sword, striking the wolves with divine force. Their malevolence dissolved into nothingness as they were consumed by the weapon's sacred energy.

They had overcome yet another perilous trial, our unity and newfound abilities proving invaluable. As they pressed on toward Kurukshetra, the looming confrontation with the resurrected asuras drew closer, and the weight of their mission bore down on them with renewed intensity.

Every step felt like an eternity, and the mist played tricks on their senses, distorting their perception of time and space. It was a test of their mental fortitude, challenging them to stay focused and resolute. They relied on the bond forged through trials and training, drawing strength from one another to navigate the disorienting maze of the enchanted forest.

As they pressed deeper into the heart of the forest, the mist grew thicker, and the very trees seemed to come alive, their branches reaching out like gnarled hands to hinder their progress. It was a relentless assault on their determination, a battle not against tangible foes but against the very essence of the forest itself.

In those moments of darkness and uncertainty, they found solace in their shared purpose and unwavering commitment to the mission. They knew that only by staying true to their path and supporting one another could they hope to emerge from the enchanted forest and face the resurrected asuras on the battlefield of Kurukshetra.

With each step, they whispered the mantra that had guided them thus far, a reminder of the divine calling that had brought them together: "Om Trimurti Devaya Namaha." It was a beacon of hope in the midst of darkness, a reminder that their journey was far from over and that the fate of humanity rested on their shoulders.

CHAPTER THIRTEEN

THE UNCHARTED TERRITORY

The mist that enveloped the group in the heart of the enchanted forest was more than a physical phenomenon; it was a test of their inner resilience. Each step they took felt like a journey through the recesses of their own minds, as doubts and fears threatened to consume them.

Preeti, her grip on Nakula's sword unwavering, was the first to confront the inner demons the mist stirred. Memories of past failures and doubts about her ability to protect her friends haunted her. But with a steely determination, she pushed through the miasma of uncertainty, drawing strength from the bonds of friendship and purpose that bound their group together.

Karthik, encased in Karna's Armor, faced his own inner struggles. The weight of his past mistakes and the burden of living up to the Armor's legacy bore down on him. But he found solace in the knowledge that he had chosen the path of redemption and that his actions on this journey would define his true character.

Tara, her powers weakened by the mystical mist, grappled with self-doubt and questioned her role in their group. She had always been the one to guide and protect, but now she felt vulnerable. Yet, she found strength in her determination to stand by her friends and fulfil her mission.

As for Akash, the mist dredged up memories of past battles and the fear of failing in their quest to protect humanity. But the teachings of Parashurama echoed in his mind, reminding him of the importance of unwavering resolve. With renewed determination, he pressed forward, knowing that the mist's true purpose was to assess their mettle.

With each step, the mist seemed to recede, gradually revealing a path forward. It was as if their inner struggles and doubts were the keys to unlocking the forest's secrets. As they continued, they discovered that the enchanted forest was not just a physical challenge but a spiritual one—an odyssey through the depths of their own souls.

In the heart of the mist-shrouded forest, they learned that their greatest adversaries were not the bewitched creatures or treacherous terrain, but the doubts and fears that resided within them. And it was through confronting and overcoming these inner demons that they found the strength to navigate the uncharted territory and emerge on the other side, ready to face the resurrected asuras and fulfil their divine mission.

The mist had served as a crucible, forging their inner resolve, and fortifying their unity as a group. With renewed purpose and a deeper understanding of themselves, they continued their journey to Kurukshetra, where the ultimate test of their mettle awaited them, and where the fate of humanity would be decided.

CHAPTER FOURTEEN

THE TEST OF RESILIENCE

The mist that enshrouded the group in the heart of the enchanted forest was more than just a physical phenomenon; it represented a profound test of their inner resilience and fortitude. Each step they took through the thick, otherworldly fog felt like a journey into the depths of their own minds, where doubts and fears threatened to consume them from within.

Preeti, her grip on Nakula's sword unwavering, confronted the inner demons that the mist stirred. Memories of past failures and nagging doubts about her ability to protect her friends haunted her thoughts. However, with a determination that burned like a beacon in the gloom of uncertainty, she pushed through the suffocating miasma of self-doubt. Drawing strength from the unbreakable bonds of friendship and the noble purpose that bound their group together, she emerged from the inner struggle with renewed resolve.

Karthik, encased in Karna's formidable Armor, grappled with his own inner turmoil. The weight of past mistakes and the burden of living up to the legacy of the Armor he bore pressed upon his shoulders. Yet, he found solace in the realization that he had chosen the path of redemption and that his actions on this perilous journey would define the true character he aspired to be. His inner battles mirrored the physical challenges he faced, and with each step, he grew stronger in spirit.

Tara, her powers weakened by the mystical mist, found herself entangled in a web of self-doubt and uncertainty. She questioned her role within their group, as she had always been the one to guide and protect. Now, vulnerable and facing her own inner demons, she grappled with her sense of self-worth. Yet, her determination to stand by her friends and fulfil her sacred mission remained unshaken, proving that strength can emerge from vulnerability.

As for Akash, the mist dredged up memories of past battles and the looming fear of failing in their quest to protect humanity. However, the teachings of Parashurama, echoing in his mind like a guiding mantra, reminded him of the paramount importance of unwavering resolve in the face of adversity. With renewed determination and a clear sense of purpose, he pressed forward, recognizing that the mist's true purpose was not only to obscure their path but also to assess the mettle of their hearts and the depth of their commitment to the mission at hand.

In the heart of the mystical forest, where the outer world and inner struggles converged, they continued their relentless journey, strengthened by the trials they had faced and the unity of purpose that bound them as chosen protectors. The mist, while formidable, served as a crucible through which their spirits were tested and refined, forging them into a group of unwavering warriors ready to face whatever challenges lay ahead on the path to Kurukshetra.

CHAPTER FIFTEEN

THE HALLOWED BATTLEGROUND

Their arduous journey had been a true test of strength, both individually and as a unified group. Along this challenging path, they had faced not only physical perils but also delved deep into the recesses of their own souls, emerging stronger and more resolute. Chosen by divine providence, they had embraced their purpose with unwavering clarity of vision – to serve as the guardians of the world, shielding humanity from malevolent asuras and preventing the shroud of darkness from descending upon the realm of mortals.

As they gazed upon the outskirts of Kurukshetra, the very ground where the forces of good and evil were destined to clash, their hearts beat in unison, resonating with a fusion of determination and trepidation. The fate of humanity teetered on a precipice, and they understood that this moment demanded their unwavering commitment, even if it meant laying down their lives in the pursuit of their noble mission.

The sun, a molten orb descending below the horizon, cast long and ominous shadows across the battlefield. Across the vast expanse, the asuras began to converge on the opposing side. The time for words had long passed; it was now a moment of resolute action and unwavering purpose.

With their legendary weapons, imbued with the ancient power of the cosmos, firmly in their grasp and their extraordinary abilities honed to perfection through relentless training, they took their positions on the battlefield. The final confrontation with the resurrected asuras loomed ominously, and the entire world seemed to hold its breath, waiting in anticipation of the impending clash.

The stage was set for a battle of epic proportions, one that would not only determine the immediate fate of humanity but also echo through the annals of history as a testament to the unwavering spirit of those who stood in the face of darkness. They, the chosen protectors, stood unwavering and resolute, prepared to confront the encroaching forces of darkness with a determination that could move mountains and a unity that was unbreakable.

CHAPTER SIXTEEN

The Clash of Titans

Under the blanket of the first twinkling stars overhead, an oppressive silence draped itself over the battlefield. The asuras, emanating malevolence that tainted the very air, assembled their dark ranks. Their leader, a grotesque and formidable figure, stepped forward, his eyes aflame with an insatiable hunger for power.

The collective breaths of the chosen protectors hung suspended in the frigid night air, visible puffs of resolute determination. One final, unspoken exchange of glances between them conveyed the profound weight of the task that lay ahead.

Then, without uttering a single word, they advanced, their footsteps echoing like the foreboding beat of a war drum.

The clash that ensued defied mortal comprehension, a titanic collision of forces beyond the scope of imagination. Akash, with the swiftness of thought, unleashed the Brahmastra, a torrent of divine energy that streaked across the night sky like a blazing comet. Its searing purity engulfed the asura leader, consuming him in a cleansing fire.

Preeti, her mastery of Nakula's sword unsurpassed, engaged in a mesmerizing dance of blades with a group of asura generals. Her every movement was a stroke of deadly artistry, each strike finding its target with exquisite precision.

Karthik, encased in the sacred Armor of Karna, became an unyielding bastion. He stood as a formidable shield, defending their flank against waves of asura foot soldiers, deflecting their most potent attacks with unwavering resolve.

Tara, her mental prowess finely honed under Parashurama's tutelage, focused her energies on the asura spellcasters. With a mere thought, she shattered their incantations and rendered their dark spells impotent, sending them spiraling harmlessly into the void.

The battle raged on, a symphony of chaos and valour, as they confronted the resurrected asuras with a unity born of their unbreakable bond. Their legendary weapons pulsed with divine might, and their abilities flowed like an unending river of power.

Yet, the asuras were no ordinary adversaries; they were ancient beings of unimaginable might. The battle-hardened warriors of antiquity clashed with them, their determination to plunge the world into darkness unwavering. The very earth quaked beneath their feet, and the very heavens seemed to hold its breath.

Amidst the heart of this tumultuous maelstrom, as the battle reached its zenith, a moment of profound clarity enveloped them. They recalled the teachings of Parashurama, the divine blessings bestowed upon them by the Trimurti, and the unwavering support of their friends and allies.

With renewed determination, they surged forward, each of them tapping into the depths of their newfound powers. The battlefield transformed into a canvas of brilliance and shadow, a testament to the timeless struggle between the forces of good and evil.

CHAPTER SEVENTEEN

THE UNLIKELY ALLY

Amidst the relentless clash between the group of chosen protectors and the resurrected asuras, a sudden disruption in the tumultuous conflict drew their collective attention. Emerging from the shadowy periphery of the battlefield was an unexpected and imposing figure. The protectors were confused but when they saw a red spot on his head shaped like a gem, they understood that he was none other than the son Dronachaarya Ashwatthama

This warrior, Ashwatthama, was garbed in battle-worn Armor that bore the marks of countless conflicts, and he carried a weapon that gleamed with deadly intent.

His face was etched with the scars of a lifetime on the battlefield, and his eyes held a depth of experience that spoke volumes.

The protectors exchanged puzzled glances, for Ashwatthama's history was deeply entwined with the very war they sought to prevent from happening again – the great Kurukshetra War. His presence on the battlefield was a revelation, and they could not immediately discern whether he had come as a friend or foe.

However, with a raised hand and a gesture, Ashwatthama made his intention clear – he desired to join their cause and fight alongside them against the resurrected Asuras. He explained that he had personally witnessed the horrors of war and had borne the heavy burden of his past actions. Now, he sought redemption by aiding their mission to prevent the asuras from wreaking havoc once more.

Ashwatthama possessed unparalleled knowledge of the Asuras' strengths and weaknesses, and his combat skills were legendary. With his deep understanding of the Asuras' tactics, he could help them strategize to counter their relentless onslaught.

While some among the protectors held reservations and skepticism about accepting Ashwatthama, they ultimately chose to embrace him as their ally. He had turned his back on his dark past and was resolute in his determination to make amends. Together, they formed an unlikely but powerful alliance, combining their unique strengths and experiences to confront the resurrected Asuras on equal footing.

Ashwatthama's presence on the battlefield became a symbol of redemption and the belief that even those with the darkest of pasts could choose the path of righteousness. With him standing alongside them, their resolve was bolstered, and the tide of battle began to shift. As the clash of titans continued, the destiny of humanity teetered on a precipice, and the outcome remained uncertain. However, with their newfound ally and the unbreakable bond that united them, they fought on with unwavering determination, fully committed to fulfilling their roles as the chosen protectors and ensuring that darkness would not prevail.

CHAPTER EIGHTEEN

THE TIDE OF BATTLE

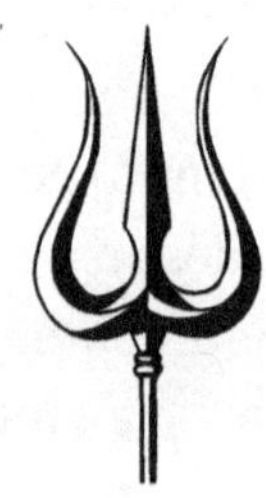

The addition of Ashwatthama, a once-feared warrior from the Kauravas' army, introduced a profound dynamic to the group of chosen protectors. His unique knowledge of the resurrected asuras and his unparalleled combat expertise made him an invaluable ally in their mission to thwart the malevolent forces threatening to engulf the world in darkness.

Under Ashwatthama's astute guidance, they crafted a comprehensive and multi-faceted battle strategy. Each member of the group had a specific role to play, capitalizing on their individual strengths and legendary weapons.

With the resonance of divine purpose in their hearts, they ventured forth to confront the Asuras on the battlefield.

Akash, armed with the formidable Brahmastra, Vaishnav Astra, and Brahmashirastra, assumed the role of the vanguard, targeting the asura leaders and striking at the heart of their command structure. With unerring accuracy, he unleashed these divine weapons, creating havoc among the asura forces and weakening their resolve.

Karthik, clad in the impervious Karna's Armor, became the unyielding frontline defender of their group. His unwavering presence shielded them from the deadliest of asura attacks, and his ability to share the Armor's protection ensured that the entire group was safeguarded from harm.

Preeti and Tara, both having honed their martial skills under the watchful eye of Parashurama, played critical roles in their strategy. Preeti, wielding Nakula's sword with unmatched precision, carved a path through the asura ranks, striking down adversaries with grace and lethal intent. Tara, with her extraordinary ability to manipulate the minds of Asuras, sowed confusion and chaos among the enemy's ranks, disrupting their formations and sapping their morale.

Despite the overwhelming power and numbers of the resurrected asuras, their unity, unwavering determination, and the strategic brilliance of Ashwatthama enabled them to turn the tide of battle in their Favor. The very earth beneath them seemed to resonate with the weight of their purpose, and the malevolent forces that had threatened to plunge the world into darkness now faltered in the face of their relentless onslaught.

As the battlefield became a chaotic maelstrom of violence and divine power clashed with malevolent fury, they could see the asuras beginning to falter. Their alliance, forged through the crucible of conflict and redemption, stood as a beacon of hope in the darkest of times. Victory, once distant, now seemed within their grasp, and the fate of humanity hung in the balance as they pressed forward with unwavering resolve.

CHAPTER NINETEEN

THE FINAL STAND

The final confrontation with the resurrected Asura leaders was an epic clash that resonated with the fate of humanity hanging in the balance. These malevolent beings, fuelled by hatred and dark intent, were determined to make their mark on the battlefield, but they faced a united front of chosen protectors armed with divine weapons and unwavering resolve.

At the heart of the battlefield, Akash squared off against the asura leader, a monstrous figure whose wings cast ominous shadows and whose eyes blazed with malice. With Gandiva, the legendary bow granted to Akash by Lord Vishnu, in his grasp, he drew upon the divine power that coursed through him. Arrows, swift as the very concept of light, filled the sky, creating a mesmerizing display of celestial destruction that sought to overwhelm and vanquish the malevolent presence before him.

Karthik, fortified by the invulnerable Karna's Armor, engaged another asura leader in a titanic clash that sent shockwaves rippling through the battlefield. Their ferocious battle served as a testament to Karthik's unwavering determination and the incredible defensive capabilities of the sacred Armor.

Preeti and Tara, their coordinated attacks a testament to their exceptional combat prowess, confronted a third asura leader. With Nakula's sword and Tara's mental manipulation powers working in perfect harmony, they became an unstoppable force, striking blow after blow against their formidable adversary.

As the battle reached its zenith, the weight of Ashwatthama's past sins seemed to pale in comparison to the redemption he had discovered on the battlefield. His martial expertise and intimate knowledge of the asuras played a pivotal role in tipping the scales in their favour.

In a climactic showdown, they systematically overcame the asura leaders one by one. Their dark powers waned, and their malevolence was extinguished in the face of the group's unwavering determination and divine might. With each fallen leader, the Asura forces weakened further, until they stood on the precipice of defeat, their once-formidable strength shattered by the united front and the blessings of the divine.

The battlefield, once a scene of chaos and darkness, now bore witness to their triumph over the forces of evil. The malevolent presence that had threatened to engulf the world was no more. Their alliance, forged in the crucible of conflict and redemption, had prevailed, and the destiny of humanity had been safeguarded from the looming shadow of the resurrected asuras. As they stood victorious amidst the aftermath of the battle, a profound sense of fulfilment and unity washed over them, a testament to the enduring power of courage, redemption, and the unwavering commitment to protecting the world from darkness.

CHAPTER TWENTY

THE HEROIC STAND

As the battle raged on the hallowed grounds of Kurukshetra, a defining moment emerged that would test the mettle of Akash and Preeti, pushing them to the limits of their abilities and the depths of their friendship.

Akash, wielding the legendary Gandiva bow and his divine arsenal, had become a beacon of hope for our group. His unparalleled archery skills allowed him to fire arrows at speeds faster than light, devastating the asura ranks. Yet, amidst the chaos of the battle, a formidable adversary arose. This asura leader possessed mastery over dark magic and illusion, conjuring shadowy phantasms that threatened to disorient and overpower Akash.

Recognizing the imminent danger, Preeti, Nakula's sword in hand, sprang into action. Her exceptional agility and combat expertise allowed her to navigate the treacherous illusions, slicing through them like a blade through the darkness. She reached Akash's side, forming an unspoken alliance forged in trust and shared purpose.

Together, Akash and Preeti melded their strengths into a seamless dance of combat. Akash maintained his relentless barrage of divine arrows, his focus honed on targeting the asura leader. Preeti, the protector, and guardian, expertly deflected the malevolent sorceries directed at them, ensuring Akash's attacks found their mark.

Their synchronization was a breathtaking display of skill and teamwork, a testament to the unbreakable bond forged through their shared trials and tribulations. Akash's arrows flew with unerring precision, striking true against the asura leader. Preeti's swordsmanship flowed seamlessly, her blade intercepting and neutralizing the dark magic hurled their way.

Their battle became a beacon of hope amidst the turmoil, a symbol of the indomitable spirit of those who stood against the encroaching darkness. They understood that the fate of humanity rested, in part, on their shoulders. With unwavering resolve and unwavering unity, they continued their heroic stand, ready to face whatever challenges lay ahead in their relentless pursuit of victory for the forces of light.

In this crucible of battle, where the clash of good and evil resounded like a thunderous symphony, Akash and Preeti embodied the essence of heroism, their unyielding commitment shining brighter than any celestial light on the battlefield.

CHAPTER TWENTY-ONE

THE SACRIFICE

As the epic battle on the hallowed grounds of Kurukshetra reached its climactic moment, Akash and Preeti faced an agonizing choice that would test their unwavering resolve and the depths of their friendship.

The Asura leader, though wounded, summoned his remaining dark powers for one final, devastating attack. A vortex of malevolent energy threatened to engulf them, promising destruction, and chaos. Akash and Preeti, standing side by side in their valiant stand, knew that they could not allow this cataclysm to be unleashed upon the world.

In an act of unparalleled selflessness, Akash made the ultimate sacrifice. Drawing upon the full extent of his divine powers, he conjured a radiant barrier of pure light that intercepted and absorbed the Asura leader's dark energy, preventing the impending catastrophe.

The strain of this selfless act was overwhelming, and Akash's strength was utterly depleted. He collapsed, his body spent, but his spirit unbroken. Preeti, torn between awe and anguish, rushed to his side. She had borne witness to her friend's incredible sacrifice and knew the immense price he had paid.

However, Akash's sacrifice was not in vain. The Asura leader, stripped of his dark powers, was left vulnerable and defenseless. With a final, resolute strike, Preeti thrust Nakula's sword through the heart of the malevolent being, ending his threat once and for all.

As the leader of the asuras crumbled to dust, an eerie silence settled upon the battlefield. The sacrifice of one had ensured the triumph of many. Akash, weakened but alive, had demonstrated the true essence of heroism, and his actions would be celebrated and remembered for generations to come.

Preeti, her heart heavy with the weight of her friend's sacrifice, knew that they had achieved victory at a tremendous cost. The world had been saved from the impending darkness, but it had come at the expense of a dear friend's well-being. As the battle-worn chosen protectors regrouped and tended to Akash's weakened form, they understood that the road ahead would be one of healing, reflection, and rebuilding. Yet, they also knew that the bond forged through their trials and sacrifices was unbreakable, and their unity would guide them through whatever challenges lay ahead.

CHAPTER TWENTY-TWO

THE TRIUMPH OF LIGHT

The aftermath of the battle on the sacred grounds of Kurukshetra was a tableau of mixed emotions. A profound stillness descended upon the once tumultuous battlefield, as the malevolent forces that had threatened to plunge the world into darkness had been vanquished.

The chosen protectors stood amidst the aftermath, triumphant but weary. The toll of the battle was evident in their every step, etched onto their faces, and weighed heavily upon their shoulders. The presence of Ashwatthama, a once-darkened warrior now redeemed, had been instrumental in securing their victory.

The world itself seemed to heave a collective sigh of relief, as if nature had been holding its breath during the climactic battle. The sacred grounds of Kurukshetra, steeped in the echoes of countless epic struggles, had borne witness to their heroic stand against the resurrected asuras.

But the cost of victory was readily apparent. Akash, who had harnessed the full might of his divine powers to defeat the asura leader, lay weakened and drained, his aura flickering like a fading star. Preeti and Tara, who had valiantly protected their flanks throughout the battle, showed signs of profound exhaustion, their eyes bearing the weight of their unwavering commitment. Even Karthik, encased in the indomitable Karna's Armor, displayed the toll that the battle had exacted.

As for Preeti, her Nakula's sword had been a symbol of precision and martial skill on the battlefield, but it had also carried with it its share of challenges and sacrifices. The scars of their arduous journey were not confined to their bodies but etched deep into the very fabric of their souls.

Victory had been achieved, but it was a victory that had left them with profound lessons and indelible marks. The world had been spared from the impending darkness, and the balance had been restored, but the price had been high. In the wake of the battle, they were left to contemplate the sacrifices made and the enduring bonds forged in the crucible of combat.

In the distance, the first rays of dawn broke, casting a warm and gentle light upon the battlefield. It was a symbol of hope and renewal, a testament to the enduring resilience of humanity and the triumph of light over darkness. As they gathered together, their chosen protectors' group, they knew that their journey was far from over, and new challenges awaited them on the path of guardianship. But for now, they stood united, their spirits undiminished, and their commitment unwavering, ready to face whatever trials lay ahead and protect the world from the shadows that threatened to encroach upon it.

REDEMPTION AND RENEWAL

The battlefield, once a chaotic maelstrom of conflict and darkness, now lay in stillness. The malevolent forces that had threatened to plunge the world into eternal night had been vanquished, their remnants dissipated like shadows before the morning sun.

Akash, though weakened by his selfless sacrifice, had emerged as a symbol of light and heroism. Preeti, Karthik, Tara, and Ashwatthama, their strengths tested to the very limit, had stood unwavering in the face of adversity.

As the first rays of dawn began to break on the horizon, a warm and hopeful light bathed the hallowed grounds of Kurukshetra. It was a new day, a day free from the looming threat of the resurrected asuras. United as the chosen protectors, they stood together, their hearts filled with a profound sense of accomplishment and sorrow. The world was safe from the darkness that had threatened to engulf it, and the triumphant spirit of hope had vanquished despair, but at the cost of their friend's life

Their journey, a gruelling odyssey marked by trials and tribulations, had forged unbreakable bonds of friendship and unity. They had confronted their inner demons and emerged stronger, more resolute in their purpose. Akash's selfless sacrifice illuminated the path of heroism, teaching them that the true measure of a hero lies in the willingness to give all for the sake of others.

With the battle won, they knew that their mission was far from over. The world remained a place filled with challenges and perils, but they were prepared to face them united in purpose. Their legacy as the chosen protectors would be one of hope, courage, and an unwavering belief that even in the darkest of times, the light of humanity could pierce through the shadows.

And so, as the sun rose on a new day, they cast their eyes toward the future with their hope and determination decreasing from each second the world would perpetually confront threats and challenges, but with the unbreakable bonds of friendship, the unyielding strength of unity, and the enduring power of heroism, they would continue to protect and safeguard humanity. The dawn of hope would forever shine brightly, a beacon for all those who believed in the indomitable spirit of the chosen protectors.

CHAPTER TWENTY-FOUR

THE DAWN OF HOPE

The sacrifice made by Akash had turned the tide of battle once and for all. With their leader defeated, the asura forces began to crumble, their malevolent power waning.

Preeti, her eyes filled with tears, cradled her fallen comrade. Akash, weakened but alive, managed a faint smile. Their friendship, forged through countless trials and tribulations, had been the bedrock of their success. But Preeti couldn't contain her emotions. She cried uncontrollably, overwhelmed by the guilt that she had somehow failed to protect Akash from harm. She believed that it was her fault that he had to make such a drastic sacrifice.

Their friends, Karthik, Tara, and Ashwatthama, gathered around them. They refused to accept the loss of their friend, knowing that there had to be a way to bring him back.

A few moments later they saw a divine light. They were astonished to see their preceptor, Parashurama. All bowed to him. He then said, his voice echoing through the battlefield "You have succeeded me and the gods, tell me what you desire, and I shall grant it". Preeti stood up and told," Guruji all we wish is to see our friend Akash alive". Parashuram replied" So be it. Go to mount Meru Scale up its heights and there you shall find Amrita to revive Akash. It is situated 42 miles west-southwest of Mount Kilimanjaro, near the Kenyan border. The extinct crater is easily accessible from Arusha town, which lies at the mountain's southern base.

Determined to save their friend, our group of chosen protectors embarked on a new journey, guided by the hope of resurrection. With heavy hearts and a steely resolve, they set out to search for the fabled artifact, knowing that the challenges ahead would be as formidable as any they had faced before.

CHAPTER TWENTY-FIVE

THE QUEST FOR REVIVAL

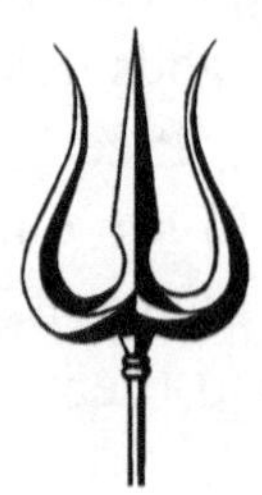

With their fallen comrade, Akash, lying in their midst, the chosen protectors set forth on a new quest - the quest for the fabled Amrita Kalasha, the vessel of immortality that held the power to bring the dead back to life. It was a journey fraught with peril, yet they were resolute in their determination to save their friend.

The pursuit of the Amrita Kalasha, the vessel containing the nectar of immortality, was a journey fraught with peril and uncertainty. The artifact's elusive location was concealed in the most remote and treacherous corners of Mount Meru, shrouded in an aura of enigma and mystique. Nevertheless, the chosen protectors remained undaunted, their determination fortified by the memory of Akash's sacrifice and the unwavering hope of his resurrection.

Their odyssey led them through dense jungles, across vast deserts, and over towering mountain ranges. Along the way, they encountered mystical beings and wise sages who imparted cryptic clues about the Amrita Kalasha's whereabouts. Each enigmatic hint brought them a step closer to their coveted goal.

Throughout their journey, they faced trials that tested their courage, wisdom, and strength. Fierce guardians challenged their worthiness to possess the nectar of immortality, subjecting them to rigorous examinations of their resolve. Every trial was a testament to their unwavering commitment and their unrelenting determination to save their fallen friend.

At last, they reached the mountain. It was a magnificent mountain. It was the great Meru which had been used for the churning of the milk ocean, the place where Lord Brahma was said to reside.

As they delved deeper into Meru, their bonds of friendship and unity grew stronger. They drew strength not only from their companions but also from the memory of their past victories. The teachings of Parashurama resonated in their hearts, serving as a guiding beacon, and reminding them of the paramount importance of virtue and selflessness.

Their quest was more than just a physical journey; it was a spiritual odyssey, a crucible of character, and a test of their unwavering belief in the power of hope. They were acutely aware that the fate of their friend and the promise of his resurrection hinged upon the success of their perilous quest.

With each arduous step they took, they inched closer to the fabled artifact that held the nectar of immortality. The challenges they faced were monumental, yet they were armed not only with their skills and abilities but also with the virtues that had marked them as chosen protectors. The quest for the Amrita Kalasha would stretch them to their limits, but they were resolute in their determination to overcome every obstacle that lay ahead.

CHAPTER TWENTY-SIX

THE PERILOUS JOURNEY

As the chosen protectors ventured deeper into uncharted territories, their quest for the elusive Amrita Kalasha transformed into a profound odyssey, one that tested not only their physical prowess but also their spiritual resilience. They confronted trials that demanded unwavering courage, profound wisdom, and indomitable endurance, with each challenge designed to probe the depths of their mettle and their unyielding commitment to rescuing their fallen friend.

In the heart of dense and unforgiving jungles, they confronted savage beasts and navigated treacherous terrain. Preeti's unparalleled combat skills, Karthik's unshakable resolve within Karna's

Armor, Tara's unyielding mental fortitude, and Ashwatthama's profound knowledge of ancient lore all played pivotal roles in guiding them through this perilous landscape.

In vast and scorching deserts, they battled not only the relentless sun but also the seemingly infinite stretches of unforgiving sands. The oppressive heat threatened to sap their strength, but their shared purpose and the memory of Akash's sacrifice propelled them forward, lending them the fortitude to endure the harshest of trials.

Scaling towering mountain peaks presented its own set of challenges—thin air, jagged cliffs, and perilous chasms tested their agility and endurance to the limits. Each step they took was not just a physical trial but also an exploration of their inner strength and their unity as a team. They understood that their quest encompassed more than just a physical journey; it was a test of their spirits and their unwavering bonds of friendship.

Throughout their arduous journey, they encountered mystical beings and wise sages who shared cryptic clues regarding the whereabouts of the Amrita Kalasha. These encounters added layers of complexity to their quest, pushing them to rely not only on their physical prowess but also on their wisdom and intuition.

With each challenge they conquered, their determination grew more resolute, and the bonds of their friendship deepened. The memory of Akash's selfless sacrifice served as a constant wellspring of inspiration, reminding them of the profound significance of their mission. The quest for the Amrita Kalasha may have been fraught with peril, but their commitment to saving their fallen comrade remained unwavering, driving them forward through every trial and tribulation.

CHAPTER TWENTY-SEVEN

THE GUARDIAN OF TIME

Their journey took an unexpected turn when they reached a realm where time itself seemed to bend and twist. Here, they encountered a guardian known as the "Keeper of Time," a being who existed beyond the constraints of mortal understanding.

The Guardian posed a challenge that transcended physical trials. They were tasked with unraveling the mysteries of time, understanding its cyclical nature, and demonstrating their ability to manipulate its flow. Tara, with her unique power to stop time for eighteen precious minutes, played a pivotal role in this trial.

Through their collective efforts and unwavering determination, they passed the test, earning the admiration of the enigmatic guardian. In return, the Keeper of Time bestowed upon them a fragment of his wisdom, a piece of knowledge that would guide them to the next step in their quest for the Amrita Kalasha.

CHAPTER TWENTY-EIGHT

THE FINAL TEST

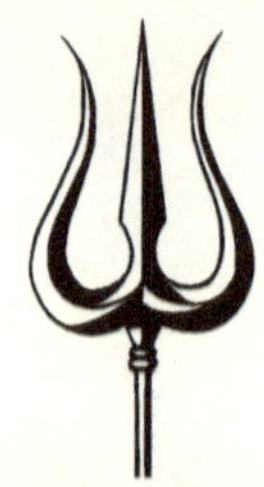

The chosen protectors, guided by the elemental wisdom and moral clarity gained from their encounters with the guardians of the elements, pressed onward toward the hidden heart of the mystical realm. Their quest had become a relentless trial of not only their physical prowess but also their spiritual mettle.

In the shadow of a towering mountain, the protectors reached their ultimate test. Here, they faced an enigmatic figure known as the Sage of the Mountain, a being whose very presence resonated with the eternal wisdom of the cosmos. He revealed that the Amrita Kalasha lay within a sacred cave high atop the peak, but only those who proved themselves virtuous and just could access it.

The Sage of the Mountain set forth the final trial, a test of character and virtue that transcended physical abilities. The protectors were presented with a choice that bore the weight of their past deeds and the destiny of their fallen friend, Akash. Each protector was called upon to confront their innermost flaws and choose between the path of righteousness or self-interest.

The moral dilemmas posed were both profound and personal, designed to challenge the very core of their beings. Would they act with selflessness, upholding the principles of virtue and sacrifice that had guided their journey, or would they succumb to temptation and abandon their moral compass?

For Preeti, the choice forced her to confront her deep-seated anger and thirst for vengeance. Karthik was challenged to choose between personal glory and the greater good. Tara grappled with a decision that touched upon her mastery of mental manipulation, while Ashwatthama's dilemma delved into the shadow of his own past actions.

As the protectors grappled with their individual moral tests, they drew strength from their collective unity and the lessons they had learned from their journey. The fate of Akash and the destiny of the world rested upon their choices. With the wisdom of the elemental guardians and the teachings of Parashurama as their guiding light, they stood on the precipice of the final trial, knowing that their decisions would determine not only their own destinies but also the very course of the world itself.

CHAPTER TWENTY-NINE

THE NEXUS OF KNOWLEDGE

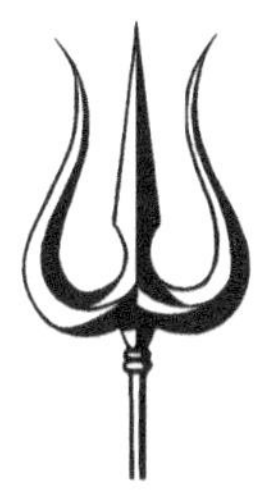

Empowered by the timeless wisdom of the Keeper of Time, the chosen protectors continued their quest for the Amrita Kalasha with newfound clarity and resolve. The challenges they had encountered thus far had tested their physical abilities, their faith, and their mastery over the elements. Now, they ventured into uncharted realms of knowledge and mysticism.

With each passing day, the memory of their fallen comrade, Akash, remained a poignant reminder of the urgency of their mission. Time was a precious commodity, and they couldn't afford to falter in their quest to resurrect their friend.

Their journey led them to the Nexus of Knowledge, a place where ancient wisdom and cosmic truths converged. Here, they encountered enigmatic beings who possessed profound insights into the mysteries of the universe. These guardians of wisdom challenged the protectors to expand their understanding of the world and their place within it.

As they delved deeper into the Nexus, the chosen protectors unlocked hidden chambers of knowledge, gaining insights into the secrets of existence and the interconnectedness of all things. They learned that the quest for the Amrita Kalasha was not just a physical journey but also a spiritual one—a journey of self-discovery and enlightenment.

The bonds of friendship and unity among the protectors grew stronger with each trial they faced. The Amrita Kalasha, the vessel of immortality, was within reach, and they were more determined than ever to bring Akash back to life and fulfil their sacred mission of protecting humanity from the forces of darkness.

In this Nexus of Knowledge, where past, present, and future converged, the chosen protectors continued their relentless pursuit of the Amrita Kalasha and the hope of resurrecting their fallen comrade. The mysteries of the universe beckoned them forward, and they were prepared to face whatever challenges lay ahead in their quest for ultimate enlightenment and the salvation of their friend.

CHAPTER THIRTY

THE COSMIC CONVERGENCE

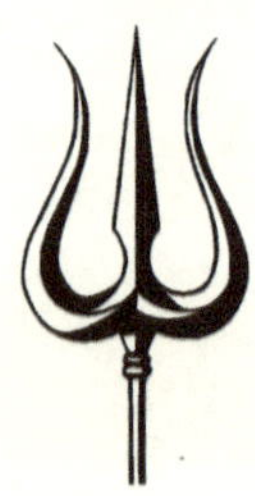

As the chosen protectors ventured further into the Nexus of Knowledge, they were enveloped in a realm where past, present, and future converged in a mesmerizing tapestry of cosmic wisdom. Here, they encountered beings of ancient wisdom and cosmic insight who would further illuminate the path to the Amrita Kalasha.

Each protector faced a unique and profound revelation, delving into the deepest recesses of their own existence and understanding. Preeti was confronted with the nature of her anger and her ultimate choice to transcend it through forgiveness. Karthik had to confront the shadow of pride and recognize the importance of humility and selflessness. Tara was tasked with understanding the intricate web of destiny and the power of

her choices in shaping it. Ashwatthama, still haunted by the ghosts of his past, had to acknowledge that redemption lay within his grasp.

The cosmic revelations empowered the chosen protectors with a heightened awareness of their connection to the universe and the role they played in the grand tapestry of existence. They learned that their journey was not merely a physical quest for the Amrita Kalasha but a spiritual odyssey that had the potential to transform them in profound ways.

Their unwavering unity, forged through trials and tribulations, and their commitment to their fallen comrade, Akash, remained a beacon of inspiration. The Amrita Kalasha was no longer an elusive dream but an attainable goal, and they were more determined than ever to bring their friend back to life and safeguard humanity from the encroaching darkness.

The chosen protectors were ready to embrace the wisdom they had gained in the Nexus of Knowledge, as they continued their relentless pursuit of the Amrita Kalasha. With the past, present, and future converging around them, they understood that their destiny was intricately entwined with the fate of the world, and they stood resolute in the face of whatever challenges lay ahead on their path to ultimate enlightenment and the salvation of their friend.

THE TRIUMPH OF VIRTUE

The chosen protectors, guided by their profound experiences and the wisdom they had gained from the time trials, ventured deeper into the heart of the mystical realm. Their quest had transformed into a spiritual odyssey, testing not only their physical abilities but also their moral character.

As they stood before the Sage of the Mountain, the enigmatic figure radiating cosmic wisdom, they confronted their most profound moral dilemmas. Each protector had to make a choice that would lay bare their true nature, determining their worthiness to access the Amrita Kalasha.

Preeti, who had grappled with a deep-seated thirst for vengeance, chose the path of forgiveness and compassion, proving that her spirit was marked by virtue. Karthik, who had been tempted by personal glory, embraced the path of selflessness, revealing the nobility of his heart. Tara, whose mastery of mental manipulation was unparalleled, chose to respect the boundaries of free will, affirming her commitment to righteousness. Ashwatthama, shadowed by his past actions, made a choice that illuminated his path of redemption and the capacity for change.

With each protector making choices that reflected their highest virtues, the Sage of the Mountain acknowledged their worthiness. He bestowed upon them his blessings and revealed the location of the sacred cave, high atop the towering peak, where the Amrita Kalasha awaited.

With the wisdom of the elemental guardians and the strength of their unwavering virtue, the protectors embarked on the final ascent. Their collective spirit, bound by friendship and unity, had guided them to this critical juncture. The memory of Akash's sacrifice and the hope of his resurrection were the driving forces behind their unwavering determination.

As they climbed toward the sacred cave, they knew that their quest was nearing its climax, and the fate of their fallen friend hung in the balance. With the lessons of their journey and their unwavering commitment to righteousness, they stood ready to face the ultimate test of their courage and resolve.

THE SACRED GROVE

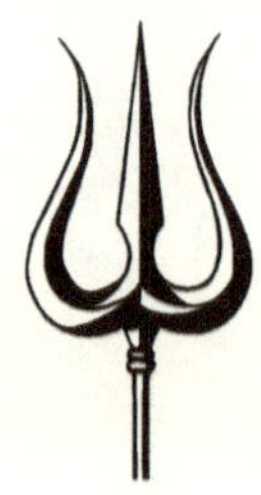

Their journey through the mystical realm, guided by the riddle's clues, had brought the chosen protectors to a place where the boundaries between the mortal world and the divine realm blurred. In this surreal dimension, reality itself seemed to shift and bend, governed by a different set of cosmic laws.

Here, they encountered celestial beings of ethereal beauty and profound power—guardians of the Amrita Kalasha. These ethereal entities subjected the chosen protectors to trials that tested the purity of their hearts, the unwavering strength of their commitment to their mission, and their willingness to make the ultimate sacrifice for the greater good.

Each protector faced a deeply personal trial that delved into their innermost fears and desires. Temptations were laid before them, promises of power, eternal life, and the ability to reshape their destinies. Yet, in the face of these seductive offers, they stood unwavering, choosing the path of selflessness and sacrifice over personal gain.

Their collective determination and unwavering resolve touched the hearts of the celestial guardians, who recognized the true essence of heroism within these mortal souls. In gratitude for their unwavering virtue, the guardians revealed the elusive location of the Amrita Kalasha—a sacred grove hidden amidst enchantments and guarded by mystical creatures of immense power.

With hearts filled with gratitude and a newfound understanding of the profound nature of heroism, the chosen protectors embarked on the final leg of their quest. Their destination was the heart of the sacred grove, where the Amrita Kalasha awaited them, and where the ultimate trial—the culmination of their epic journey—loomed ominously.

The fate of their dear friend, Akash, hung in the balance, and the realization of their mission to resurrect him was within their grasp as they ventured toward the sacred grove. With the weight of their entire journey pressing upon them, they steeled themselves for the final and most perilous trial that awaited them. This was the moment they had been tirelessly working towards—the climax of their epic odyssey.

The story of the chosen protectors, their unwavering commitment, and their unbreakable bonds was about to reach its zenith, and the destiny of Akash and the world itself teetered on the precipice of revelation.

CHAPTER THIRTY-THREE

THE TRIALS OF THE SACRED GROVE

The sacred grove was a realm of surreal beauty and profound mystique, where the chosen protectors found themselves in the final and most perilous trial of their epic journey. As they ventured deeper into this enchanting sanctuary, the atmosphere resonated with an aura of cosmic significance.

Amidst the lush, vibrant foliage of the sacred grove, they encountered celestial beings of divine grace and profound power—guardians who watched over the Amrita Kalasha, the vessel of immortality. These ethereal entities tested the resolve and virtue of the protectors in a series of trials, each designed to probe the depths of their character and their unwavering commitment to their mission.

In the first trial, Preeti was confronted with a vision of a world plagued by chaos and darkness. She was offered the power to quell this turmoil but at the cost of forsaking her quest to resurrect Akash. Her unyielding spirit chose the path of selflessness, reaffirming her commitment to her dear friend.

In the second trial, Karthik was presented with the allure of wielding god-like power, enabling him to rewrite the course of his own destiny. Yet, he understood that the essence of heroism lay in humility and sacrifice, and he rejected this temptation with resolute determination.

Tara, in the third trial, was offered the knowledge of the fates of those around her. The weight of this burden would allow her to navigate life with ease but would strip her of her own free will. Her unshakable willpower and the lessons learned from her journey guided her to reject this offer.

The fourth trial confronted Ashwatthama with the memory of his past actions and the torment he had inflicted upon the world. He was offered the chance to erase this dark history, but he recognized that redemption lay in atoning for his past rather than erasing it.

In the culmination of these trials, the celestial guardians were moved by the chosen protectors' unwavering virtue, strength, and selflessness. In recognition of their true heroism, the guardians shared the location of the Amrita Kalasha and the path to its sanctum, where the nectar of immortality awaited.

With hearts filled with gratitude and a profound understanding of the essence of heroism, the chosen protectors moved onward, determined to seize the opportunity to resurrect their fallen comrade, Akash. They faced the final and most perilous trial, one that would require every ounce of their strength and unity. The destiny of their dear friend and the fate of the world rested on the precipice of revelation, and the conclusion of their epic odyssey was imminent.

CHAPTER THIRTY-FOUR

The Amazing Return to Life

With excitement and nervousness, the chosen protectors faced the magical Amrita Kalasha, a container with the power of immortality. It glowed brightly, and a sense of something incredible about to happen filled the air.

Getting their hands on the Amrita Kalasha wasn't easy. It was well-guarded, surrounded by powerful enchantments, and protected by a massive celestial guardian – a being with incredible strength and wisdom.

The celestial guardian, seeing their pure intentions and the sacrifices they'd made on their journey, gave them one last challenge. This challenge was like a puzzle, testing how well they understood life, death, and the idea of living forever.

Together, the protectors discussed and came up with an answer. This was a moment of deep truth, the climax of their journey, and proof of their unwavering determination to bring back their fallen friend, Akash.

The celestial guardian was pleased with their response. They gave them access to the Amrita Kalasha, and with hearts full of hope and respect, they approached the magical container, ready to perform a special ceremony that could defy the rules of life and death.

In a solemn and almost magical ritual, they used the Amrita Kalasha's power. It shimmered with an otherworldly light, covering Akash's lifeless body. It felt like time itself was holding its breath as the extraordinary process of bringing him back to life began.

Slowly, Akash started to stir. His face regained its colour, and it became clear that he was coming back to the world of the living. The chosen protectors watched in amazement and gratitude. Their friend, who had made great sacrifices for their mission, was returning from the edge of death.

As Akash opened his eyes, a mix of wonder and confusion filled his face. He saw the faces of the friends who had risked everything to save him. In this miraculous moment, their bond of friendship and unity grew even stronger.

Their journey, filled with challenges, sacrifices, and unwavering friendship, had reached its peak. The chosen protectors had defied the natural order to rescue their friend. Their story would be remembered for generations to come, shining as a symbol of hope.

With Akash back among them, the group was whole again, ready to face any future challenges. Their epic adventure had come to an end, but their strong commitment to protecting humanity from dark forces would always guide them.

As they looked at their friend, who had returned to life, their hearts swelled with gratitude and a deep sense of fulfilment. The world was safe, and their friend had been given a second chance at life. This showed the incredible power of friendship, sacrifice, and the unwavering spirit of the chosen protectors.

Part 2 - The Never-Ending Journey

CHAPTER THIRTY-FIVE

A Fresh Start

The world had changed forever because of the brave chosen protectors. Their incredible journey, starting with the intense battle against the resurrected Asuras and leading to their quest for the Amrita Kalasha to bring Akash back, had become a story that people would tell for generations. It gave hope and inspiration to all who heard it.

The chosen protectors had defeated the evil forces that tried to bring darkness to the world. They had become heroes, admired by everyone. Their story was shared by storytellers and singers in villages and towns, and people everywhere knew their names. They were seen as symbols of bravery and togetherness.

But being heroes didn't mean their journey had ended. The world was still full of surprises and challenges. They weren't chosen just for one battle; they were meant to protect humanity from dark forces for their whole lives.

The strong friendships they had built during their adventures were still as powerful as ever. Each protector brought their unique abilities and experiences to the group, and their trust in each other was unbreakable. They had faced some of the toughest challenges together, and it had made them even stronger.

Looking ahead, the chosen protectors were filled with bravery and determination. They knew the world would always need protectors, and they were ready to step up. With their strong commitment and the lessons, they'd learned during their tough journey, they were ready for whatever challenges were waiting for them.

Their legacy was all about bravery, togetherness, and the belief that even in the darkest times, hope would always win. As the new day started, the chosen protectors were watchful, determined, and unshakable, always ready to safeguard humanity from any darkness that might try to harm the world.

CHAPTER THIRTY-SIX

A TIME FOR LOOKING BACK

In a peaceful garden, surrounded by the calm beauty of nature, the chosen protectors paused to think about their amazing journey. Preeti, her eyes filled with the wisdom they'd gained from their adventures, shared her thoughts on how important it was to be brave when facing tough times. She talked about how strength comes not from hiding your weaknesses but from being open about them. Preeti also mentioned the strong bond of friendship that had helped them through their hardest moments.

Karthik, speaking with confidence, added his reflections. He spoke about how a person can change and find a better path, even after making big mistakes. Karthik had carried the weight of his past errors, but with the help of his fellow protectors and their shared mission, he'd found a way to make amends. His journey taught him that the choices we make today can create a brighter tomorrow for everyone.

Tara, who had a deep understanding of people's minds, shared her thoughts about the personal struggles they'd faced on their journey. She talked about the importance of believing in yourself and finding the strength to conquer your doubts and fears. Tara's experiences strengthened her resolve to protect the world from darkness, and she encouraged her friends to find their inner strength.

Ashwatthama, once a feared warrior who'd found a path to change, talked about how everyone deserves a second chance. He spoke about the importance of admitting your past mistakes and choosing a different way forward. His presence among them was proof that people can change and grow. He inspired his fellow protectors to aim for their best selves.

Together, they thought about the tough challenges and sacrifices they'd faced and the strong bonds they'd built. Their journey hadn't just saved the world from a big threat; it had also made them better people. In the calm of the garden, they found peace and strength in each other's company. They knew their mission to protect humanity would go on with their strong commitment and unity.

CHAPTER THIRTY-SEVEN

THE POWER OF STAYING TOGETHER

The chosen protectors sat in the peaceful garden, and their words carried the wisdom of their shared adventures. Ashwatthama, once a feared warrior, spoke of how he had transformed into a better person. He highlighted the importance of forgiving oneself and leaving a dark past behind to create a brighter future.

Akash, who had returned from the edge of death, shared his deep insights about how all life is connected. He talked about how there's endless potential for change and growth. Akash emphasized the significance of selflessness and how unity brings enduring strength.

Their words touched everyone deeply, reinforcing the unbreakable bond that had formed among the protectors during their challenging journey. The garden, with its lovely flowers and the soothing sound of flowing water, became a special place for them to think and refresh their spirits.

As they sat together, surrounded by the calming beauty of nature, they knew their mission to protect humanity was not over. They looked to the future with hopeful hearts, ready to face whatever challenges came their way. The lessons they'd learned—like finding courage during tough times, the power of making amends, the strength of believing in themselves, and the transformative nature of unity—would continue to guide them in their ongoing quest to protect humanity from the forces of darkness.

A Rekindled Purpose

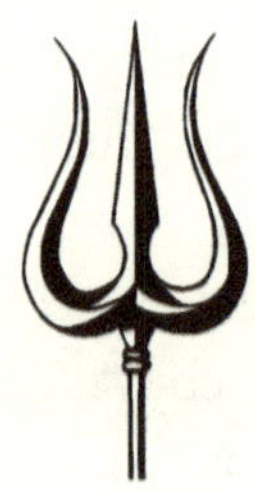

With a profound sense of duty ignited within them, the chosen protectors stood shoulder to shoulder, ready to confront whatever challenges lay ahead. Their epic journey had imprinted valuable lessons on their hearts, teaching them the importance of working together, making sacrifices, and putting others before themselves.

They understood that their mission to protect humanity was not limited by time or circumstance. As long as threats loomed over the world, they would stand as its steadfast defenders. With their unbreakable bond and unwavering determination, they were committed to being a source of hope and the guardians of peace in a world that continually relied on their protection.

THE RESURGENCE OF DARKNESS

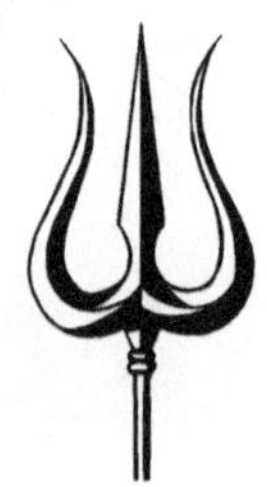

In the garden, now bathed in the gentle, warm light of the setting sun, a sense of peace and determination filled the air. The chosen protectors had not only saved their world from evil forces but had also undergone a deep transformation themselves.

Their journey had taught them that real strength goes beyond physical abilities. It's found in the connections they've built, their readiness to make selfless sacrifices for the greater good, and their belief in the possibility of redemption, even from the darkest past.

As they stood on the edge of an uncertain future, their hearts were brimming with hope, and their minds enriched with profound wisdom. Their unity remained unshakable. The lessons they'd learned and the experiences they'd shared would continue to guide them. Together, they were determined to be unwavering protectors of humanity, ready to preserve the light in a world that sometimes faces darkness.

CHAPTER FORTY

A Gathering Storm

Their journey through the unforgiving terrain had been a testament to their unwavering determination and newfound wisdom. Despite the harshest challenges, they emerged stronger, individually and as a united front.

When facing the remnants of the resurrected asuras, they did so with a renewed sense of purpose and unity that had only grown stronger since their previous battle. Their legendary weapons brimmed with divine power, their abilities flowed like a ceaseless river of strength, and their hearts were filled with the understanding that they were humanity's relentless protectors.

With each hard-earned victory, their dedication to shield their world from the forces of darkness deepened. They recognized that their journey was continuous, and the world would always encounter threats. However, with their unwavering bond and resolute determination, they were ready to serve as a symbol of hope and unwavering strength in the face of any adversity.

CHAPTER FORTY-ONE

A GLIMMER OF HOPE

The cryptic prophecy found on the ancient tablet served as a catalyst, propelling the chosen protectors into immediate action. With indomitable spirits and an unquenchable thirst for knowledge, they set out to decipher the mysterious clues that would lead them to their potential ally.

Their journey took them through mystical realms and uncharted territories, where they encountered beings of unparalleled power and wisdom. Each encounter brought them a step closer to unravelling the mystery of their newfound ally's identity and the critical role this ally would play in the impending battle against the forces of darkness.

The challenges they faced during this journey tested not only their physical strength but also their intellect and adaptability. The numerous battles they had fought had honed their combat skills, but now they needed to apply their wisdom and resourcefulness to navigate the intricate complexities of the realms they explored.

With each revelation and obstacle overcome, the chosen protectors grew more resolute in their determination to secure the alliance of their enigmatic ally. They understood that not only the fate of their world but also the very essence of light and hope hung precariously in the balance. They were willing to exert every ounce of effort and courage needed to tip the scales in favour of the forces of good.

CHAPTER FORTY-TWO

UNVEILING HIDDEN TRUTHS

In a concealed realm, the chosen protectors delved deeper into the complexities of the cosmic convergence. They discovered a troubling reality: the impending catastrophe didn't just threaten their world but the entire multiverse. Its origins could be traced back to a powerful entity determined to disrupt the delicate balance between creation and destruction. These actions had set off a dangerous chain of events, endangering the very fabric of reality.

Guided by immensely wise and powerful beings, the chosen protectors learned that the potential ally they sought was no ordinary being. This ally was a cosmic guardian, a being with unparalleled knowledge of ancient cosmic forces and the ability to control them. Their role was to preserve the equilibrium of the multiverse, ensuring that creation and destruction remained in perfect harmony.

This revelation expanded the chosen protectors' understanding of the monumental task ahead of them. Their mission was much more significant and far-reaching than they had initially realized. They needed to find and convince the cosmic guardian to join their cause, uniting the cosmic forces of creation and destruction to prevent the impending catastrophe.

With this new knowledge, their journey transcended the boundaries of their own world and extended into the vast multiverse. Here, they would face unimaginable challenges and confront the very essence of cosmic power and destiny. The fate of not only their world but countless others hung in the balance as they embarked on this epic quest to save all of existence.

To be continued...

www.ingramcontent.com/pod-product-compliance
Lightning Source LLC
Chambersburg PA
CBHW022013150726
47990CB00002B/638